Dommy B has won New York's famous
Nuyorican Poetry Cafe Slam and UK's
Superheroes of Slam. He has performed his
poetry on BBC's *Rhyme Rocket*.

The Story of Spark, the Goblin Wizard is
adapted from his own poetry theatre show
for children aged 5+ and their families.

THE STORY OF SPARK THE GOBLIN WIZARD

DOMMY B

Flapjack Press
flapjackpress.co.uk

Published in 2014 by Flapjack Press
Chiffon Way, Salford, Gtr Manchester
flapjackpress.co.uk

Reprinted in 2015

ISBN 978-0-9576639-2-3

Puzzles designed & drawn by the author
Cover & illustrations by Brink
paulneads.co.uk

Printed by Lonsdale Direct
Denington Estate, Wellingborough, Northants
lonsdaledirect.co.uk

Supported by
The Hamilton Project
thehamiltonproject.co.uk

CONTENTS

Dedicated to Mum.
Thank you for always bringing magic into my life. X

CHAPTER ONE
A GOBLIN SONG

Do you know the songs of the woods?
Of werewolves and girls in red hoods?
Of gingerbread homes?
Of fairies and gnomes?
Do you know the songs of the woods?

Do you know who live underground
and hide where they cannot be found?
Beneath the tree roots
who feast on the fruits?
Do you know who live underground?

Have you seen a goblin before?
Come closer and I'll tell you more.
They live out of sight,
roam mostly by night.
Have you seen a goblin before?

For this is a wood goblin song.
They're tiny but crafty and strong.
So think what might be
just under that tree,
for this is a wood goblin song...

Goblins are small, scaly, slimy creatures with sharp fangs and long claws.

There is one thing that scares goblins more than anything else. Goblins are really,

really,

scared

of...

...people!

Yeah! People! Isn't that weird?

A goblin would be *really* scared of *you*!

Seriously, if a goblin saw *you*, a goblin would say...

"AAAAA
AAAAAA
AAAAAA
AAAAAA

☆

AAAAAA

AAAAAAA

AAAAAAA

ARGH!"

Isn't that silly?

This is a story about a goblin that lives in an enchanted forest and is a very powerful magician.

This is the story of Spark, the goblin wizard.

CHAPTER TWO
MEET THE GOBLIN WIZARD

Spark, the goblin wizard,
looks like a hairy lizard.
This furry beast excels
at casting magic spells.

He'll turn the bogeys up his nose
into some pink ribbons and bows.
He'll turn the dirt between toenails
into a ship with satin sails.
He'll turn his burps (that smell horrific)
into cake - that tastes terrific!

Spark the goblin wizard
is mighty as a blizzard
and sharp as a bee sting.
He'll transform anything!

He'll make a gorgeous high-heeled shoe
out of a pile of donkey poo.
He'll make a lovely summer hat
out of a freshly laid cow pat.
He'll make meringues with whipped cream toppings
out of fox and rabbit droppings.

Spark the goblin wizard
looks like a hairy lizard.
This furry beast excels
at casting magic spells.

There's one thing goblins fear.
They will never go near
people. You and me!
That's why I doubt you'll see

in a city or park
by day or after dark
this goblin make his mark...
the goblin wizard... Spark.

CHAPTER THREE

WHY ARE GOBLINS SCARED OF PEOPLE?

Why *are* goblins scared of people?

Well, the truth is... these goblins have never even *spoken* to a person. Sometimes they hide in shadows between the trees and watch while people pass.

But because people *talk* so differently to goblins, and because people *walk* so differently to goblins, and because people *look* so different to goblins, goblins think goblins and people are *too different* to ever be friends. And goblins think anyone who isn't a friend... must be their enemy.

That's why goblins are scared of people.

CHAPTER FOUR

A VERY WISE GRANDMOTHER

Spark lives in a small burrow beneath a crooked and gnarled oak tree. He lives there with his crooked and gnarled Grandmother.

Now, if I called *my* Grandmother crooked and gnarled, I don't think she'd be very pleased with me (I don't think you *are* crooked and gnarled, Nan, I think you are *lovely*).

Spark's Grandmother thinks that being called crooked and gnarled *is* lovely. Telling a goblin you think that they are crooked and gnarled is like telling a person you think that they are very clever, or really kind, or that you like their new jumper.

Spark's Grandmother says the same wise thing to Spark every single morning of every single day. First thing every day she says, "Bwbwbwbwbwbwbw! Spark! The kinder a wizard is, the more powerful a wizard is. The kinder you are, the stronger your magic will be. Bwbwbwbwbwbwbw!"

Then, every day, Spark uses his spells to magically transform things found lying about the forest (acorns, twigs, leaves) into fantastic food (cakes, curries, burgers) on which he and his Grandmother feast.

Then they eat and burp and eat and burp and eat and burp.

When Spark's Grandmother burps, she burps the wisest burps in all the forest.

CHAPTER FIVE

A VISIT FROM THE GOBLIN LEADER

One day, Spark is home alone. His Grandmother has gone out to play bingo with the silver haired mermaids of Great Gala Lake. Spark is sat on his own when he hears a loud knock on his door. He slowly gets up to see who it is.

You can tell how important a goblin is just by looking at that goblin.

The more ear wax that a goblin has drooling out its ears, the more important that goblin is.

If you *smell* a goblin's ear wax... and that goblin's ear wax smells like... sweaty... mouldy... stinky, old cheese... that has been sat on... by a skunk... for three and a half years... well, only *the most* important goblins smell like that.

Spark opens his door to see the Goblin Leader stood before him. The Goblin Leader is *the most important* goblin and so, of course, has the *smelliest* ear wax *ever*. A smell *so strong* one whiff could knock out a whole army of highly trained dung beetles.

"Please, help me, Spark," she begs. "I fell into a wasps' nest and some nasty wasps have stung me on my bottom. Can you please, please, please transform anything into some... *bottom ointment*? Please!"

Spark claps his hands, rubs his palms together and says...

"No! I'm too busy. Sorry."

He kicks out the Goblin Leader with her poor, sore bottom and slams his door shut.

The truth is, Spark isn't busy. He's just feeling lazy. With his Grandmother out he knows he can get away with doing *nothing* and instead enjoy a morning nap.

CHAPTER SIX

A VISIT FROM A WEREWOLF CALLED TWINKLE TOES

Later that morning, Spark's Grandmother is still not back when there is another knock at the door. Annoyed to be woken up from his nap, Spark grumpily gets up to see who has come to bother him this time.

He opens his door to find a poor, young goblin girl has come to visit. She has brought her pet werewolf. A werewolf called Twinkle Toes.

"GRRRRRRRRRRRRR," says Twinkle Toes.

"Please, sir," she asks, "I'm so very poor and Twinkle Toes is so, so, so hungry. Please, could you transform anything into some *food* for Twinkle Toes... please? Maybe some cake, or curries, or burgers? Twinkle Toes eats anything."

"GRRRRRRRRRRRRRRRRRRRRRRR," says Twinkle Toes, staring hungrily at Spark and licking his massive lips.

Spark claps his hands, rubs his palms together and says...

"No! I'm too busy. Sorry."

Twinkle Toes leaves hungry and Spark has another nap.

CHAPTER SEVEN
A FLYING CARPET AND SOME JAM

Much, much, much, much, much later that day Spark's Grandmother *still* isn't back. Spark decides to go out and about around the forest.

Spark's far too lazy to walk anywhere though, so he has an idea - he'll transform something into a flying carpet.

"What can I transform into a flying carpet...? I know! I don't need this *bottom ointment*. I've had this bottom ointment in my cupboard for *years* and I've never needed to use it. Who would need bottom ointment anyway? I think I'll transform it into a flying carpet."

Everyone knows all magic spells have to rhyme.

Here is the spell Spark uses to transform one thing into something else:

"A hiss of snake,
a werewolf's bark,
transform for me,
transform for Spark!"

Spark wiggles his fingers as he speaks these words. A burst of blue smoke puffs up into the air and the bottom ointment transforms into... a flying carpet.

Spark leaps onto the flying carpet and flies all around the forest. He is having a great time, nipping in between the trees, zipping back and forth all over the place, until he starts to feel... a bit hungry.

He decides to transform one of the trees into a tasty, jam sandwich.

"A hiss of snake,
a werewolf's bark,
transform for me,
transform for Spark!"

However... something *unexpected* happens.

The tree does *not* become a tasty, jam sandwich.

The tree transforms into one enormous lump of raspberry jam the size of a baby elephant.

Splat!

The flying carpet rams into the jam. Spark is knocked off and falls face first into the jammy lump.

Squelch!

"Ugh!" splutters Spark. "My magic didn't work! Why didn't my magic work? Never mind. I will just cast a spell to transform this jam back into a tree. No problem.

A hiss of snake,
a werewolf's bark,
transform for me,
transform for Spark!"

It doesn't work.

Instead, *two more* trees transform into jam and fall down onto Spark's head.

Splat! Splat!

Spark tries to cast another spell, but before he can another *twenty eight* trees turn into jam and drop down on top of him.

Splat! Splat!

... Splat!

Spark is trapped under jam – unable to move!

"Help!" he calls. "Help! I'm stuck! *Help!*"

Spark shouts and shouts and shouts until his throat is hoarse and he can shout no more.

When he stops shouting he hears a faint noise coming from far, far away.

BUZZ BUZZ BUZZ

"Wasps!" screams Spark. "Wasps are coming! Wasps are coming and I can't move! This is an emergency! I need to cast - *the - most - powerful* there is. The most powerful spell Grandmother taught me - a spell that transforms really, really *nasty* things into... really, really *lovely* things!"

CHAPTER EIGHT

THE WORDS TO THE MOST POWERFUL SPELL

Make it *nice*.
Make it *nice*.
Nice as a big pizza slice.
Nice as ice cream. Say it twice.
Make it *nice*.
Make it *nice*.

Shake this nasty feeling off,
don't want to hurt and ache.
I want to make things lovely
like a massive chocolate cake.
I want to make things lovely
like the sunshine after showers.
I want to make things lovely
like a big bouquet of flowers.
I want to make things lovely
and I really don't know how,
I want to make things lovely
and I want it lovely now!

Make it *nice*.
Make it *nice*.
Nice as a big pizza slice.
Nice as ice cream. Say it twice.

Make it *nice*.
Make it *nice*.

Shake this nasty feeling off,
please make it go away.
I want to make things lovely
like a perfect holiday.
I want to make things lovely,
just as lovely as can be -
like I'm swimming in the sky
or flying through the sea.
I want to make things lovely
like a lovely kitty cat.
I want to make things lovely
'cos lovely is where it's at!

Make it *nice*.
Make it *nice*.
Nice as a big pizza slice.
Nice as ice cream. Say it *thrice*.
Make it *nice*.
Make it *nice*.
Make
it
NICE...

A hiss of snake,
a werewolf's bark,
transform for me,
transform for Spark!

CHAPTER NINE

WASPS ARE FOUND AND CHILDREN ARE LOST

Hundreds and hundreds of fierce wasps hover over Spark's head.

The wasps have not transformed into cake.

The wasps have not transformed into kitty cats.

The wasps all... dive into the jam!

Every time one bumps into Spark it gives him a little sting.

"Ow! Ow! Owwww! Gerroff! Gerroff!"

After the wasps have eaten as much as they can they slowly buzz away, rubbing their bulging tummies and enjoying big, jammy burps.

Spark is still stuck, but now he's not only stuck, he's covered in wasp stings.

"Why isn't my magic working?" sobs Spark. "Will anyone ever find me? Grandmother...? Goblin Leader...? Anybody...? Somebody help me, please!"

At that point, somebody does appear. In fact, several people appear... several *human* children.

When Spark sees them he says...

"AAAAA

AAAAAA

AAAAAA

AAAAAA

AAAAAA

AAAAAA

AAAAAA

ARGH!"

But the children can see Spark is stuck, hurt and sad.
They feel sorry for him and, despite his ear-splitting
screaming, they all roll up their sleeves and start to dig
through the jam in an effort to try and free him.

CHAPTER TEN
HOW TO GET HOME

The children stop digging. Spark is free!

"Um, um... thank you?" mumbles Spark, still a little bit frightened of his saviours.

Suddenly all of the other goblins jump out from the shadows between the trees. They had been hiding there the whole time.

"Who are you?" they shout fearfully at the children. "Why are you in our forest?"

"We were playing in the forest," explains one of the children nervously, "and we got lost. We don't know how to get back home."

The goblins start to quieten down. These people are smaller than any they have seen before. They don't seem to be any threat. And they *did* just help Spark...

"If my magic worked, I would magic you home," says Spark. "But my magic has stopped working. None of my magic works."

Just then everyone hears a different voice.

"Bwbwbwbwbwbwbw!"

It's Spark's Grandmother!

"Bwbwbwbwbwbwbwbw! Spark! The kinder a wizard is, the more powerful a wizard is. The kinder you are, the stronger your magic will be. Bwbwbwbwbwbwbw!"

"You can do it, Spark," the Goblin Leader encourages. "This act of kindness will bring your magic powers back, I am sure."

"GRRRRRRRRRRRR," says Twinkle Toes.

"OK." Spark takes a deep breath. "I'll try my best. Here we go!"

CHAPTER ELEVEN

A NEW SPELL

Now Spark, the goblin wizard,
needs to find a rhyme that's new.
A rhyme that's so exciting
you will not know what to do,
to make you dance about just like
you really need the loo...
so you'll be hopping round as if
you're desperate for a poo!

Yes, Spark the goblin wizard,
needs to find a rhyme that's new.
A rhyme that's so exciting
and is full of kindness too.
Then he will make a carpet fly,
I promise you, it's true!
Then all the children will fly home
and shout a loud *WOO HOO!*

CHAPTER TWELVE
MAGIC FOR EVERYONE

When Spark wiggles his fingers and speaks these words, a burst of blue smoke puffs up into the air.

The grass beneath the children's feet transforms into... a massive flying carpet to fly all the children out of the forest and safely back home!

"Bye!" all the children shout, waving down at the goblins. "Thank you, Spark!"

Spark promises that he will not use magic just to help himself, but to help all of his friends.

He transforms loads of acorns, twigs and leaves into cakes, curries and burgers for Twinkle Toes the werewolf to eat.

"GRRRRRRRRRRRYUMYUMYUM," says Twinkle Toes.

(If you have been wondering whether the story might end with Twinkle Toes eating Spark, well, Twinkle Toes was wondering the same thing. Cake tastes much nicer than goblin though.)

As much as Spark loves his flying carpet, he transforms it back into bottom ointment for the Goblin Leader. He decides her happiness is more important than his luxuries.

For his Grandmother, Spark transforms a pile of broken branches into a glistening trophy. On the trophy is written:

FOR THE MOST CROOKED AND GNARLED GOBLIN EVER. THIS AWARD IS FOR THE BEST BURPS I HAVE EVER HEARD.

The children come back to the forest many times to visit Spark. He uses his magic to transform bushes and rivers into trampolines and water slides for him and the children to play on.

Spark still thinks that goblins and people are very different to each other, but he has learnt that not only can they get along together, they can even become the very best of friends.

PUZZLES AND GAMES
THE STOLEN SPELLS, PART ONE

One day, Spark and his Grandmother wake to find out that their book of spells has been stolen!

"I know who the thief is," Spark tells his Grandmother. "My sworn enemy, Blast the dragon, must have crept in during the night and stolen it whilst we slept. Grandmother, we have to get our book back!"

Can you guide Spark and his Grandmother from **START** up through the maze to Blast's cave?

When you reach an arrow, you can only pass in the direction that the arrow is pointing. You cannot pass an arrow if it is pointing towards you.

Don't get stuck!

ONE WAY

ONE WAY ONE WAY

START

PUZZLES AND GAMES
WICKED WORDSEARCH ONE

Can you find all of the words hidden in this puzzle?

```
                    I Z
                  N X S M
                M A A R G Q
              M G U O P R D M
            E B S F B N A C P A
          I O L S U L A N T V H J
        L V I N R Z W G D D A Z T L
      K W M A P A P K O M E H I J A M
    M O Y R O B X W N B O L L T W V L C
  Q Y T T S C A L Y I L T D G R W D R P T
  G V J A R J O E N C I H N S X A O A W S
    A Q H L C R S O E N E D S P O N I C
      H D B S X S P J M R G B K Q N G
        G V O P N D S B S Z E C K H
          H E X A W H A S D X L A
            M G H R Z U W Y E G
              U H U K E P T P
                K U R D O B
                  Z H E B
                    S X
```

SPARK	SCALY	TWINKLETOES	JAM
GOBLIN	GRANDMOTHER	BURP	SPLAT
WOODS	CROOKED	NAP	WASPS
SLIMY	GNARLED	TRANSFORM	NICE

PUZZLES AND GAMES
THE STOLEN SPELLS, PART TWO

Spark and his Grandmother make it to Blast the Dragon's hideout.

"We must stay alert, Spark!" warns his Grandmother as they cautiously tiptoe inside.

There is no sign of Blast anywhere. After much searching they find their book buried in a huge pile of gold, diamonds and emeralds.

Suddenly they hear a loud growl from the entrance to the cave. Blast is back!

Spark and his Grandmother open the spell book to find a spell with which to battle their enemy. However, the book's pages have been scorched by dragon flame and are now hard to read.

Can you help the goblins guess the last word in each rhyme before Blast attacks?

Wizard, wizard,
take a look
through the pages
of this _ _ _ _ _.
Learn these lessons
very well
and you'll cast a
magic _ _ _ _ _.
Summon up an
icy breeze
and your enemy will
_ _ _ _ _!

PUZZLES AND GAMES
CRAFTY CROSSWORD

Can you solve all these clues and complete the
crossword puzzle?

Across:

1. He is our hero! _ _ _ _ _ , the goblin wizard. (5)

4. Blast the dragon is *not* Spark's friend. Blast is Spark's
sworn _ _ _ _ _. (5)

5. Spark knows he will beat Blast sooner or _ _ _ _ _. (5)

8. Spark likes to pile loads of food on his _ _ _ _ _. (5)

Down:

1. A goblin wizard knows how to cast a magic _ _ _ _ _. (5)

2. When they enter Blast's hideout, Spark's Grandmother
warns that they must stay _ _ _ _ _. (5)

3. Spark wants to put his spell book in a box and lock it
with a _ _ _. (3)

6. Blast the dragon is greedy. A little is not enough. Blast
wants to have it _ _ _. (3)

7. Spark can also be greedy. He likes a lot to drink and
_ _ _. (3)

¹		²		³
	■		■	
⁴				
	■		■	■
⁵	⁶		⁷	
■		■		■
⁸				

THE STOLEN SPELLS, PART THREE

"Who dares trespass into my realm?" bellows Blast. The roof of the cave shudders with the force of the monster's roar. The dragon stands between the goblins and their only way out.

Can you spell out the right word that will help them pass the beast?

Guide Spark and his Grandmother from **START** up towards Blast. You cannot jump over or miss out any letters.

If you do not spell out the right word the spell will not work... and the goblins will be stuck!

If you do spell out the right word our heroes can get away!

WICKED WORDSEARCH TWO

In this puzzle are many secret, hidden words.
Are you able to find them all?

```
                    L K
                    J R
                  K N L B
                  E Q A G
                T P M I U S
                L D L Y K D
I B D R A Z I W A T D H S R L P H O A L
J O P F M C V U F N C X R C V C Y K R E
  E B U A M B A T B G L W W I N C O C
    I O G U R M O R X U O S N P M G
      E I C E O S F O R A U T E E
        C S K H E S D P F G O J
        A R C B N A S P G H P E A X
        E K Y Q Y R V T E P Y H V P
      V B W D N V C E O R L C M M B L
      P U Z Z L E H    F O L Q F A X
    U A C H E O K        C N K P W G P
    N E R Y Q              G Z R X I
  A F Z P                    H E X H
  Z B                          C Q
```

WIZARD	LANGUAGE	POEM	STRONG
MAGIC	WORD	EPIC	TROPHY
SPELL	VERSE	CRAFTY	SEARCH
BOOK	RHYME	FUNNY	PUZZLE

PUZZLES AND GAMES
THE STOLEN SPELLS, PART FOUR

Blast the dragon is frozen. Spark and his Grandmother hurry out of the cave.

"Spark, the 'FREEZE' spell won't last long!" warns his Grandmother. "We should transform something into a flying carpet to get us home quickly."

Spark agrees and transforms a small pile of pebbles into a flying carpet.

Can you get the goblins home?

Guide Spark and his Grandmother from **START** down towards **YOU WIN!**, one bubble at a time.

You must count in order from 1 to 10 without missing out or repeating any numbers.

Exhausted, Spark and his Grandmother finally arrive back at their burrow. They have retrieved their spell book and the day is saved!

"I will make sure this book is locked away somewhere safe," promises Spark. "It will be protected by goblin guards all day and night."

"What an adventure!" laughs his Grandmother. "Blast will not dare come here again!

    A hiss of snake.
    A werewolf's bark.
    Hooray, hooray,
    hooray for Spark!"

THE END

PUZZLES AND GAMES
ANSWERS

The Stolen Spells, Part One:

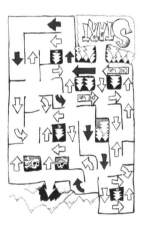

Wicked Wordsearch One:

The Stolen Spells, Part Two:

Crafty Crossword:

Wicked Wordsearch Two:

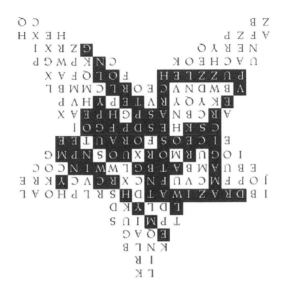

The Stolen Spells, Part Three:

The Stolen Spells, Part Four: